Stranger Fro

Hannes Bok

Alpha Editions

This edition published in 2024

ISBN : 9789362997159

Design and Setting By
Alpha Editions
www.alphaedis.com
Email - info@alphaedis.com

As per information held with us this book is in Public Domain.
This book is a reproduction of an important historical work. Alpha Editions uses the best technology to reproduce historical work in the same manner it was first published to preserve its original nature. Any marks or number seen are left intentionally to preserve its true form.

STRANGER FROM SPACE

By HANNES BOK

She prayed that a God would come from the skies and carry her away to bright adventures. But when he came in a metal globe, she knew only disappointment—for his godliness was oddly strange!

It was twilight on Venus—the rusty red that the eyes notice when their closed lids are raised to light. Against the glow, fantastically twisted trees spread claws of spiky leaves, and a group of clay huts thrust up sharp edges of shadow, like the abandoned toy blocks of a gigantic child. There was no sign of clear sky and stars—the heavens were roofed by a perpetual ceiling of dust-clouds.

A light glimmered in one of the huts. Feminine voices rippled across the clearing and into the jungle. There was laughter, then someone's faint and wistful sigh. One of the voices mourned, in the twittering Venusian speech, "How I envy you, Koroby! I wish I were being married tonight, like you!"

Koroby stared defiantly at the laughing faces of her bridesmaids. She shrugged hopelessly. "I don't care," she said slowly. "It will be nice to have Yasak for a husband—yes. And perhaps I do love him. I don't know." She tightened her lips as she reflected on it.

She left them, moving gracefully to the door. Venus-girls were generally of truly elfin proportions, so delicately slim that they seemed incapable of the slightest exertion. But Koroby's body was—compared to her friends'—voluptuous.

She rested against the door-frame, watching the red of the afterglow deepen to purple. "I want romance," she said, so softly that the girls had to strain forward to hear her. "I wish that there were other worlds than this—and that someone would drop out of the skies and claim me ... and take me away from here, away from all this—this monotony!"

She turned back to her friends, went to them, one of her hands, patting the head of the kneeling one. She eyed herself in the mirror.

"Well—heigh-ho! There don't seem to be any other worlds, and nobody is going to steal me away from Yasak, so I might as well get on with my preparations. The men with the litter will be here soon to carry me to the Stone City."

She ran slim hands down her sides, smoothing the blue sarong; she fondled her dark braids. "Trossa, how about some flowers at my ears—or do you think that it would look a little too much—?" Her eyes sought the mirror, and her lips parted in an irreprehensible smile. She trilled softly to herself, "Yes, I am beautiful tonight—the loveliest woman Yasak will ever see!" And then, regretfully, sullenly, "But oh, if only *He* would come ... the man of my dreams!"

There was a rap at the doorway; they turned. One of the litter-bearers loomed darker than the gloomy sky. "Are you ready?" he asked.

Koroby twirled before the mirror, criticizing her appearance. "Yes, ready," she said.

"Ready!" the girls cried. Then there was a little silence.

"Shall we go now?" Koroby asked, and the litter-carrier nodded. Koroby kissed the girls, one after another. "Here, Shonka—you can have this bracelet you've always liked. And this is for you, Lolla. And here, Trossa—and you, Shia. Goodbye, darlings, goodbye—come and see me whenever you can!"

"Goodbye, Koroby!"

"Goodbye! Goodbye!" They crowded around her, embracing, babbling farewells, shreds of advice. Trossa began to cry. Finally Koroby broke away from them, went to the door. She took a last look at the interior of the little hut, dim in the lamplight—at the hard bed of laced *gnau*-hide strips, the crude but beautifully-carved charts and chests. Then she turned and stepped out into the night.

"This way," the litter-carrier announced, touching the girl's arm. They stumbled over the rutted clearing toward the twinkling sparks that were the lights of the other litter-bearers, colored sparks as befitted a wedding-conveyance. The winking lights were enclosed in shells of colored glass for another reason—the danger of their firing the papery jungle verdure.

It was not a new litter, built especially for the occasion—Yasak was too practical a man to sanction any kind of waste. It was the same old litter that Koroby had been watching come and go ever since she was a little girl, a canopied framework of gaudily-painted carvings. She had wondered, watching it pass, whether its cushioned floor was soft, and now, as she stepped into the litter, she patted the padding experimentally. Yes, it was soft .... And fragrant, too—a shade too fragrant. It smelled stale, hinting of other occupants, other brides being borne to other weddings....

Garlands of flowers occupied a good deal of space in it. Settled among them, she felt like a bird in a strange nest. She leaned back among them; they rustled dryly. Too bad—it had been such a dry year—

"You're comfortable?" the litter bearer asked. Koroby nodded, and the litter was lifted, was carried along the path.

The procession filed into the jungle, into a tunnel of arched branches, of elephant-eared leaves. Above the monotonous music came the hiss of the torches, the occasional startled cry of a wakened bird. The glow of the flames, in the dusty air, hung around the party, sharply defined, like a cloak of light.

At times a breeze would shake the ceiling of foliage, producing the sound of rolling surf.

Koroby fingered the flowers around her throat, her eyes rapt on the passing trees. Her lips moved in the barest murmur: "If only—!" and again, "Oh, if only—!" But the music trickled on, and nothing happened; the litter seemed to float along—none of the bearers even stumbled.

They came to a cleared space of waist-high grass. It was like a canyon steeply walled by cliffs of verdure. The litter jerked as it glided along, and Koroby heard one of the bearers exclaim gruffly, "Listen!" Then the litter resumed its dream-like floating on the backs of the men.

"What was it?" another bearer asked.

"Thought I heard something," the other replied. "Shrill and high—like something screaming—"

Koroby peered out. "A *gnau*?" she asked.

"I don't know," the bearer volunteered.

Koroby lifted a hand. "Stop the litter," she said.

The conveyance halted. Koroby leaning out, the men peering around them, they listened. One of the bearers shouted at the musicians; the music ceased. There was nothing to be heard except the whisper of the breeze in the grass.

Then the girl heard it—a shrill, distant whine, dying away, then growing louder—and louder—it seemed to be approaching—from the sky—

All the faces were lifted up now, worriedly. The whine grew louder—Koroby's hands clenched nervously on the wreaths at her throat—

Then, far ahead, a series of bright flashes, like the lightning of the dust-storms, but brilliantly green. A silence, then staccatto reports, certainly not thunder—unlike any sound that Koroby had ever heard.

There was a babble of voices as the musicians crowded together, asking what had it been, and where—just exactly—could one suppose it had happened, that thunder—was it going to storm!

They waited, but nothing further happened—there were no more stabs of green light nor detonations. The bearers stooped to lift the litter's poles to their shoulders. "Shall we go on?" one of them asked Koroby.

She waved a hand. "Yes, go on."

The litter resumed its gentle swaying, but the music did not start again. Then, from the direction of the light-flashes, a glow appeared, shining steadily, green as the flashes had been. Noticing it, Koroby frowned. Then the path bent, and the glow swung to one side.

Suddenly Koroby reached out, tapped the shoulder of the closet bearer. "Go toward the light."

His face swung up to hers. "But—there's no path that way—"

"I don't care," she said. "Take me there." Her order had reached the others' ears, and they slowed their pace.

"Lady—believe me—it's impossible. There's nothing but matted jungle in that direction—we'd have to hack our way as we go along. And who knows how far away that light is? Besides, you're on your way to be married."

"Take me to that light!" she persisted.

They set the litter down. "We can't do that," one man said to another.

Koroby stepped out to the path, straightened up, her eyes on the glow. "You'd better," she said ominously. "Otherwise, I'll make a complaint to Yasak—"

The men eyed each other, mentally shrugging. "Well—" one yielded.

The girl whirled impatiently on the others. "Hurry!" she cried. "If you won't take me, I'll go by myself. I must get to that fire, whatever it is!" She put a hand to her heart. "I must! I must!" Then she faced the green glare again, smiling to herself.

"You can't do that!" a carrier cried.

"Well, then, you take me," she said over her shoulder.

Grumbling, they bent to the conveyance's poles, and Koroby lithely slipped to the cushions. They turned off the path, plodded through the deep grass toward the light. The litter lurched violently as their feet caught in the tangled grass, and clouds of fine dust arose from the disturbed blades.

By the time they reached the source of the light, they were quite demoralized. The musicians had not accompanied them, preferring to carry the message to Yasak in the Stone City that his prospective bride had gone off on a mad journey. The bearers were powdered grey with dust, striped with blood where the dry grass-stems had cut them. They were exhausted and panting. Koroby was walking beside them, for they had abandoned the litter finally. Her blue drapery was ripped and rumpled; her carefully-arranged braids had fallen loose; dust on her face had hid its youthful color, aging her.

The expedition emerged from the jungle on a sandy stretch of barren land. A thousand feet away a gigantic metal object lay on the sand, crumpled as though it had dropped from a great distance. It had been globular before the crash, and was pierced with holes like windows. What could it possibly be? A house? But whoever heard of a metal house? Why, who could forge such a thing! Yasak's house in the City had iron doors, and they were considered one of the most wonderful things of the age. It would take a giant to make such a ponderous thing as this.

A house, fallen from the sky? The green lights poured out of its crumpled part, and a strange bubbling and hissing filled the air.

Koroby stopped short, clasping her hands and involuntarily uttering a squeal of joyful excitement, for between her and the blaze, his eyes on the destruction, stood a man.....

He was very tall, and his shoulders were very wide. Oh, but he looked like a man, and stood like one—even though his hands were folded behind his back and he was probably dejected. A man in a house from the sky—

Koroby hastily grasped a corner of her gown, moistened it with saliva, and scrubbed her face. She rearranged her hair, and stepped forward.

"Don't go there—it's magic—he'll cast a spell—!" one of the bearers whispered urgently, reaching after her, but Koroby pushed him away. The litter-carriers watched the girl go, unconsciously huddling together as if feeling the need for combined strength. They withdrew into the jungle's shadows, and waited there anxiously, ready at any moment to run away.

But Koroby, with supreme confidence, walked toward the stranger, her lovely body graceful as a cat's, her face radiant. The man did not hear her. She halted behind him, waited silent, expectant, excited—but he did not turn. The green fire sputtered upward. At last the girl stepped to the man's side and gently touched him again. He turned, and her heart faltered: she swayed with bliss.

He was probably a god. Not even handsome Yasak looked like this. Here was a face so finely-chiseled, so perfectly proportioned, that it was almost frightening, unhuman, mechanical. It was unlined and without expression, somehow unreal. Mysterious, compelling.

He was clothed very peculiarly. A wonderfully-made metallic garment enclosed his whole body—legs and all, unlike the Venus-men's tunics. Even his feet were covered. Perhaps it was armor—though the Venus-men usually wore only breastplate and greaves. And a helmet hid all of the man's head except his face. Around his waist was a belt with many incomprehensible objects dangling from it. If he was so well armored, why was he not carrying a sword—a dagger at least! Of what use were those things on his belt—for instance, that notched L-shaped thing? It would not even make a decent club!

The stranger did not speak, merely gazed deeply into Koroby's eyes. And she, returning the gaze, wondered if he was peering into her very soul. The words of a folk-ballad came to her:

"—He'll smile and touch my cheek,

And maybe more;

And though we'll neither speak,

We'll know the score—"

Suddenly he put his hands to her cheeks and bent close to her, his eyes peering into hers as though he were searching for something he had lost in them. She spoke her thought: "What are you doing? You seem to be reading my mind!"

Without removing hands, he nodded. "Reading—mind." He stared long into her eyes. His dispassionate, too-perfect face began to frighten her. She slipped back from him, her hand clutching her throat.

He straightened up and spoke—haltingly at first, then with growing assurance. "Don't be afraid. I mean you no harm." She trembled. It was such a wonderful voice—it was as she had always dreamed it! But she had never really believed in the dream....

He was looking at the wrecked globe of metal. "So there are people on Venus!" he said slowly.

Koroby watched him, forgot her fear, and went eagerly to him, took his arm. "Who are you?" she asked. "Tell me your name!"

He turned his mask of a face to her. "My name? I have none," he said.

"No name? But who are you? Where are you from? And what is that?" She pointed at the metal globe.

"The vehicle by which I came here from a land beyond the sky," he said. She had no concept of stars or space, and he could not fully explain. "From a world known as Terra."

She was silent a moment, stunned. So there was another world! Then she asked, "Is it far? Have you come to take me there?"

Here the similarity between her dream and actual experience ended. What was he thinking as he eyed her for a long moment? She had no way of guessing. He said, "No, I am not going to take you back there." Her mouth gaped in surprise, and he continued, "As for the distance to Terra—it is incredibly far away."

The glare was beginning to die, the green flames' hissing fading to a whisper. They watched the melting globe sag on the sand. Then Koroby said, "But if it is so far away, how could you speak my language? There are some tribes beyond the jungle whose language is unlike ours—"

"I read your mind," he explained indifferently. "I have a remarkable memory."

"Remarkable indeed!" she mocked. "No one here could do that."

"But my race is infinitely superior to yours," he said blandly. "You little people—ah—" He gestured airily.

Her lips tightened and her eyes narrowed. "And I?"

His voice sounded almost surprised. "What about you?"

"You see nothing about me worthy of your respect? Are you infinitely superior to me—*me*?"

He looked her up and down. "Of course!"

Her eyes jerked wide open and she took a deep breath. "And just who do you think you are? A god?"

He shook his head. "No. Just better informed, for one thing. And—"

Koroby cut him short. "What's your name?"

"I have none."

"What do you mean, you have none?"

He seemed just a trifle bored. "We gave up names long ago on my world. We are concerned with more weighty things than our own selves. But I have a personal problem now," he said, making a peculiar sound that was not quite a sigh. "Here I am stranded on Venus, my ship utterly wrecked, and I'm due at the Reisezek Convention in two weeks. You"—he gripped Koroby's shoulder, and his strength made her wince—"tell me, where is the nearest city? I must communicate with my people at once."

She pointed. "The Stone City's that way."

"Good," he said. "Let's go there."

They took another glance at the metal globe and the green fire, which by now had died to a fitful glimmer. Then the stranger and the girl started toward the jungle, where the litter-bearers awaited them.

As the party was struggling through the prairie's tall grass, the man said to Koroby, "I realize from the pictures in your mind that there is no means in your city of communicating directly with my people. But it seems that there are materials which I can utilize in building a signal—"

He was walking along, head erect, apparently quite at ease, while the litter bearers and Koroby could barely drag themselves with him. The girl's garment was a tattered ruin. Her skin was gritty with dust, and she was bleeding from many scratches. She tripped over tangled roots and exclaimed in pain. Then the man took one of the strange implements from his belt, pressed a knob on it, and light appeared as if by magic! He handed the stick to Koroby, but she was afraid to touch it. This was a strange light that gave no heat, nor flickered in the breeze. Finally she accepted it from him, but carried it gingerly at arm's length.

She refused to believe that he had no name, and so he named himself. "Call me Robert. It is an ancient name on Terra."

"Robert," she said, and, "Robert."

But at last she could go no farther. She had forced herself along because she wanted to impress this indifferent man that she was not as inferior as he might think—but now she could not go on. With a little cry almost of relief, she sank to the ground and lay semi-conscious, so weary that the very pain of it seemed on the point of pleasure.

Robert dipped down, scooped her up, and carried her.

Lights glimmered ahead; shouts reached them. It was a searching party, Yasak in it. The litter-carriers who could still speak blurted out what had happened. "A green light—loud sounds—fire—this man there—" and then dropped into sleep.

"Someone carry these men," Yasak ordered. To Robert he said, "We're not very far from the path to the City now. Shall I carry the girl?"

"It makes no difference," Robert said.

"You will stay with me while you are in the City, of course," Yasak said, as they walked. He eyed this handsome stranger speculatively, and then turned to shout an necessary order. "You, there, keep in line!" He glanced at Robert furtively to see if this had impressed him at all.

It was day. Koroby sat up in bed and scanned her surroundings. She was in Yasak's house. The bed was very soft, the coverlets of the finest weave. The furniture was elegantly carved and painted; there were even paintings on the walls.

A woman came to the bed. She was stocky and wore drab grey: the blue circles tattooed on her cheeks proclaimed her a slave. "How do you feel?" she asked.

"Fairly well. How long have I been ill?" Koroby asked, sweetly weak.

"You haven't been ill. They brought you in last night."

"Oh," Koroby said disappointedly, and sat upright. "I feel as if I'd been lying here for weeks. Where's Yasak? Where's the strange man in armor?"

"Yasak's out somewhere. The stranger man is in the room at the end of the hall."

"Fetch me something to wear—that's good enough," the girl accepted the mantle offered by the slave. "Quick, some water—I must wash."

In a few minutes she was lightly running down the hall; she knocked on the door of Robert's room. "May I come in?"

He did not answer. She waited a little and went in. He was seated on one of the carved chairs, fussing over some scraps of metal on the table. He did not look up.

"Thank you for carrying me, Robert." He did not reply. "Robert—I dreamed of you last night. I dreamed you built another round house and that we both flew away in it. Yasak had to stay behind, and he was furious. Robert! Aren't you listening?"

"I hear you."

"Don't you think it was an exciting dream?" He shook his head. "But why? Robert"—she laid longing hands on his shoulders—"can't you see that I'm in love with you?" He shrugged. "I believe you don't know what love is!"

"I had a faint idea of it when I looked into your mind," he said. "I'm afraid I haven't any use for it. Where I come from there is no love, and there shouldn't be here, either. It's a waste of time."

"Robert—I'm mad about you! I've dreamed of your coming—all my life! Don't be so cruel—so cold to me! You mock me, say that I'm nothing, that I'm not worthy of you—"

She stepped back from him, clenching her hands. "Oh, I hate you—hate you! You don't care the least bit about me—and I've shamed myself in front of you—I, supposed to be Yasak's wife by now!" She began to cry, hid her face in suddenly lax fingers. She looked up fiercely. "I could kill you!" Robert stood immobile, no trace of feeling marring the perfection of his face. "I could kill you, and I will kill you!" she sprang at him.

"You'll hurt yourself," he admonished kindly, and after she had pummeled his chest, bruising her fingers on his armor, she turned away.

"And now if you're through playing your incomprehensible little scene," Robert said, "I hope you will excuse me. I regret that I have no emotions—I was never allowed them. But it is an esthetic regret.... I must go back to my wrecked ship now and arrange the signals there." He did not wait for her leave, but strode out of the room.

Koroby huddled on a chair, sobbing. Then she dried her eyes on the backs of her hands. She went to the narrow slits that served as windows and unfastened the translucent shutter of one. Down in the City street, Robert was walking away. Her eyes hardened, and her fingers spread into ugly claws. Without bothering to pull the shutter in place she hurried out of the room, ran eagerly down the hall. She stopped at the armor-rack at the main hall on her way outside, and snatched up a *siatcha*—a firestone. Then she slipped outside and down the street.

The City's wall was not far behind. Robert was visible in the distance, striding toward his sky-ship, a widening cloud of dust rising behind him like the spreading wake of a boat. Koroby stood on tip-toe, waving and calling after him, "Robert! Robert! Come back!" but he did not seem to hear.

She watched him a little longer. Then she deliberately stooped and drew the firestone out of its sheath. She touched it to a blade of the tall grass. A little orange flame licked up, slowly quested along the blade, down to the ground and up another stem. It slipped over to another stem, and another, growing larger, hotter—Koroby stepped back from the writhing fire, her hand protectively over her face.

The flames crackled at first—like the crumpling of thin paper. Then, as they widened and began climbing hand over hand up an invisible ladder, they roared. Koroby was running back toward the City now, away from the heat. The fire spread in a long line over the prairie. Above its roar came shouts from the City. The flames rose in a monstrous twisting pillar, brighter than even the dust-palled sky, lighting the buildings and the prairie. The heat was dreadful.

Koroby reached the City wall, panted through the gate into a shrieking crowd. Someone grasped her roughly—she was too breathless to do more than gasp for air—and shook her violently. "You fool, you utter fool! What did you think you were doing?" Others clamored around her, reaching for her. Then she heard Yasak's voice. Face stern, he pushed through the crowd, pressed her to him. "Let her alone—Let her alone, I say!"

They watched the conflagration, Yasak and Koroby, from a higher part of the wall than where the others were gathered. They could glimpse Robert now and then. He was running, trying to outrace the flames. Then they swept around him, circling him—his arms flailed frantically.

The fire had passed over the horizon. The air was blue with smoke, difficult to breathe, and ashes were drifting lightly down like dove-colored snow. Yasak, watery eyed, a cloth pressed to his nose, was walking with several others over the smoking earth and still warm ashes up to his knees. In one hand he held a stick. He stopped and pointed. "He fell about here," he said, and began to probe the ashes with the stick.

He struck something. "Here he is!" he cried. The others hurried to the spot and scooped ashes away, dog-fashion, until Robert's remains were laid clear. There were exclamations of amazement and perplexity from the people.

It was a metal skeleton, and the fragments of complicated machinery, caked with soot.

"He wasn't human at all!" Yasak marvelled. "He was some kind of a toy made to look like a man—that's why he wore armor, and his face never changed expression—"

"Magic!" someone cried, and backed away.

"Magic!" the others repeated, and edged back ... and that was the end of one of those robots which had been fashioned as servants for Terrestial men, made in Man's likeness to appease Man's vanity, then conquered him.

Milton Keynes UK
Ingram Content Group UK Ltd.
UKHW030845141124
451205UK00005B/486